Monster's Night

Level 4F

Written by Becky Davies
Illustrated by Michael Emmerson

What is synthetic phonics?

Synthetic phonics teaches children to recognise the sounds of letters and to blend (synthesise) them together to make whole words.

Understanding sound/letter relationships gives children the confidence and ability to read unfamiliar words, without having to rely on memory or guesswork; this helps them to progress towards independent reading.

Did you know? Spoken English uses more than 40 speech sounds. Each sound is called a *phoneme*. Some phonemes relate to a single letter (d-o-g) and others to combinations of letters (sh-ar-p). When a phoneme is written down it is called a *grapheme*. Teaching these sounds, matching them to their written form and sounding out words for reading is the basis of synthetic phonics.

Consultant

I love reading phonics has been created in consultation with language expert Abigail Steel. She has a background in teaching and teacher training and is a respected expert in the field of synthetic phonics. Abigail Steel is a regular contributor to educational publications. Her international education consultancy supports parents and teachers in the promotion of literacy skills.

Reading tips

This book focuses on the igh sound, made with the letters igh, as in light.

Tricky words in this book

Any words in bold may have unusual spellings or are new and have not yet been introduced.

Tricky words in this book:

try growls enough climbs roars birds does turn knight

Extra ways to have fun with this book

After the reader has read the story, ask them questions about what they have just read:

Can you remember three words that contain the igh sound?

What was Big Monster scared of?

I'm a knight, I'm not scared of anything... ARGH!

A pronunciation guide

This grid contains the sounds used in the stories in levels 4, 5 and 6 and a guide on how to say them. /a/ represents the sounds made, rather than the letters in a word.

/ai/ as in game	/ai/ as in play/they	/ee/ as in leaf/these	/ee/ as in he
/igh/ as in kite/light	/igh/ as in find/sky	/oa/ as in home	/oa/ as in snow
/oa/ as in cold	/y+oo/ as in cube/music/new	long /oo/ as in flute/crew/blue	/oi/ as in boy
/er/ as in bird/hurt	/or/ as in snore/oar/door	/or/ as in dawn/sauce/walk	/e/ as in head
/e/ as in said/any	/ou/ as in cow	/u/ as in touch	/air/ as in hare/bear/there
/eer/ as in deer/here/cashier	/t/ as in tripped/skipped	/d/ as in rained	/j/ as in gent/gin/gym
/j/ as in barge/hedge	/s/ as in cent/circus/cyst	/s/ as in prince	/s/ as in house
/ch/ as in itch/catch	/w/ as in white	/h/ as in who	/r/ as in write/rhino

Sounds this story focuses on are highlighted in the grid.

/f/ as in phone	**/f/** as in rough	**/ul/** as in pencil/ hospital	**/z/** as in fries/ cheese/breeze
/n/ as in knot/ gnome/engine	**/m/** as in welcome /thumb/column	**/g/** as in guitar/ghost	**/zh/** as in vision/beige
/k/ as in chord	**/k/** as in plaque/ bouquet	**/nk/** as in uncle	**/ks/** as in box/books/ ducks/cakes
/a/ and **/o/** as in hat/what	**/e/** and **/ee/** as in bed/he	**/i/** and **/igh/** as in fin/find	**/o/** and **/oa/** as in hot/cold
/u/ and short **/oo/** as in but/put	**/ee/**, **/e/** and **/ai/** as in eat/ bread/break	**/igh/**, **/ee/** and **/e/** as in tie/field/friend	**/ou/** and **/oa/** as in cow/blow
/ou/, **/oa/** and **/oo/** as in out/ shoulder/could	**/i/** and **/ai/** as in money/they	**/c/** and **/s/** as in cat/cent	**/y/**, **/igh/** and **/i/** as in yes/sky/myth
/g/ and **/j/** as in got/giant	**/ch/**, **/c/** and **/ sh/** as in chin/ school/chef	**/er/**, **/air/** and **/eer/** as in earth/bear/ears	**/u/**, **/ou/** and **/oa/** as in plough/dough

Be careful not to add an 'uh' sound to 's', 't', 'p', 'c', 'h', 'r', 'm', 'd', 'g', 'l', 'f' and 'b'. For example, say 'fff' not 'fuh' and 'sss' not 'suh'.

On bright, sunny days, Big
Monster is the most frightening
of all the monsters!

Nothing seems to frighten him!

Little Monster sighs.

Try as he might, he just
cannot be as scary or brave
as Big Monster.

Big Monster lurks out of sight
and **growls**. He is scary **enough**
to frighten a **knight**!

He **climbs** up high
and **roars**.

He scares all of the **birds** mid-flight!

Little Monster is too frightened
to join in.

He **does** not feel brave at all.

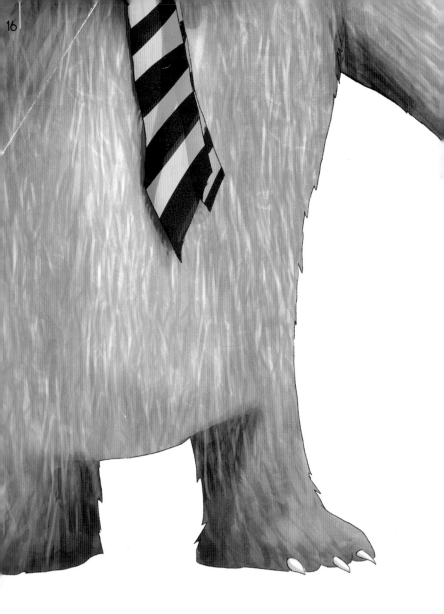

So Big Monster holds his
hand tightly,

and tells him that everything
will be all right.

At night, the monsters are
tucked up in bed.

But Big Monster is too scared to **turn** off the light!

So Little Monster holds
his hand tightly,

and tells him that everything
will be all right.

Little Monster may not be frightening, but he is brave after all...

brave at night!

OVER **48** TITLES IN SIX LEVELS
Abigail Steel recommends...

Other titles to enjoy from Level 4

I love reading phonics — **The Circus Mice**
978-1-84898-582-7

I love reading phonics — **Jemima the Spy**
978-1-84898-584-1

I love reading phonics — **The Mummy Code**
978-1-84898-585-8

Some titles from Level 5

I love reading phonics — **The Gigantic Bear**
978-1-84898-586-5

I love reading phonics — **Celebrity Celia**
978-1-84898-587-2

I love reading phonics — **The Cemetery Dance**
978-1-84898-588-9

Some titles from Level 6

I love reading phonics — **Hugh is New**
978-1-84898-590-2

I love reading phonics — **Clumsy Eagle**
978-1-84898-591-9

I love reading phonics — **Bad Zombie Movie**
978-1-84898-592-6

An Hachette UK Company
www.hachette.co.uk

Copyright © Octopus Publishing Group Ltd 2012
First published in Great Britain in 2012 by TickTock, an imprint of Octopus Publishing Group Ltd,
Endeavour House, 189 Shaftesbury Avenue, London WC2H 8JY.
www.octopusbooks.co.uk

ISBN 978 1 84898 583 4

Printed and bound in China
10 9 8 7 6 5 4 3 2 1